Inside The Mind

Edited By Andrew Porter

First published in Great Britain in 2023 by:

Young Writers
Remus House
Coltsfoot Drive
Peterborough
PE2 9BF
Telephone: 01733 890066
Website: www.youngwriters.co.uk

All Rights Reserved
Book Design by Ashley Janson
© Copyright Contributors 2022
Softback ISBN 978-1-80459-324-0

Printed and bound in the UK by BookPrintingUK
Website: www.bookprintinguk.com
YB0529N

FOREWORD

Since 1991, here at Young Writers we have celebrated the awesome power of creative writing, especially in young adults where it can serve as a vital method of expressing their emotions and views about the world around them. In every poem we see the effort and thought that each student published in this book has put into their work and by creating this anthology we hope to encourage them further with the ultimate goal of sparking a life-long love of writing.

Our latest competition for secondary school students, **The Power of Poetry,** challenged young writers to consider what was important to them and how to express that using the power of words. We wanted to give them a voice, the chance to express themselves freely and honestly, something which is so important for these young adults to feel confident and listened to. They could give an opinion, highlight an issue, consider a dilemma, impart advice or simply write about something they love. There were no restrictions on style or subject so you will find an anthology brimming with a variety of poetic styles and topics. We hope you find it as absorbing as we have.

We encourage young writers to express themselves and address subjects that matter to them, which sometimes means writing about sensitive or contentious topics. If you have been affected by any issues raised in this book, details on where to find help can be found at
www.youngwriters.co.uk/info/other/contact-lines

CONTENTS

Archbishop Sentamu Academy, Hull

Charlie-Philip Spencer (11)	1
Drew Hayes (11)	2
Phoebe Holmes (11)	3
Dylan Burke-McGlone (12)	4
Henley Whalen (11)	5
Maisie Briggs (11)	6
Adam McCracken (12)	7
Paighton Potter-McDaid (11)	8
Ellis Fewlass (11)	9
Natans Peips (12)	10
Kai Walton (11)	11
Jaden Harrison (11)	12
Laceymarie Matthews (11)	13
Arminas Stankevičius (11)	14
Lennon Shipley (12)	15
Corey Bolton (12)	16
Ryan Foster (11)	17
Eddie Robshaw (11)	18
Alfie Thundercliffe (11)	19
Jamie Hall (12)	20
Caiden Penney (11)	21

Cyfarthfa High School, Merthyr Tydfil

Rachel Cooper (12)	22
Freddie Davies (11)	24
Faith Ison (13)	26
Emilie Halloway (12)	27
Logan Jenkins (12)	28
Maddie Moule (12)	29
Nancy Gordon (11)	30
Olivia Atherton	31

Katie James (12)	32
Darcie Edwards (12)	34
Isabella Phillips (11)	35
Evan Walker (11)	36
Scarlett James (11)	37
Samuel Cole (11)	38
Summer Simons (13)	39
Jake Williams (11)	40
Olivia Jones (12)	41
Nasko Ognyanov (12)	42
Macsen Williams (11)	44
Caitlin Davies	45
Oliver Powell (11)	46
Chloe Gordon (13)	47
Jacob Burton (13)	48
Jessica Craze (14)	49
Chloe Harding (11)	50
Olivia Kaczynska (14)	51
Skye Lewis (12)	52
Lily-Beth McGovern (12)	53
Josh Billingsley (11)	54
Ethan Jenkins (12)	55
George Davies (11)	56
Ellie Pearce (11)	57
Emily Sullivan (11)	58
Will Mackie (13)	59
Emilia Jones (11)	60
Dylan Hughes (12)	61
Addison Pulman (11)	62
Reese Gray (12)	63
Lucas O'Neill (12)	64
Alfie Williams (11)	65

Excelsior Academy, Newcastle Upon Tyne

Susie Wasielewska (12)	66
Yasmeen Khalaf (11)	68
Rejoice Akenvwa (12)	70
Erfan Jadari (11)	72
Nusrat Karim (14)	74
Danielle Faichen (13)	76
James Dixon (12)	77
Summer Rose Forster (13)	78
Melissa Milova (12)	80
Maddison Palmer (11)	81
Daniel Lowdon (11)	82
Tamara Potter (13)	83
Fatima Ethni (12)	84
Thenuk Themiya Kodithuwakku (11)	85
Freya Rodmell (11)	86
Richard Pina (13)	87
Joseph Bowes (13)	88
Aiden Lee Murray (11)	89
Lauren White (13)	90
Crystabel Agbonwaneten (11)	91
Miley Humble (12)	92
Waqar Rahman (11)	94
Charlie Todd (11)	95
Azlan Zahidi (14)	96
Elisha Waterston (11)	97
Albaz Mohammed (11)	98
Stephanie Chapim (11)	99
Will Sharp (11)	100
Habiba Sultana (11)	101
Damon Graham (11)	102
Zaima Azad (11)	103
Tia-Faith Ferguson (11)	104
Kaine Wilkinson (14)	105
Grace Igo (12)	106
Musfirah Usman (11)	107
Terri Leigh Murray (13)	108
Corey Burn (13)	109
Rosie Dickinson (11)	110
Mia Stevens (12)	111
Justin Lakatos (13)	112
Mohammed Ibrahim Komal (11)	113
Muhammad-Ans Ali (11)	114
Ayesha Wilkinson (11)	115
Ethan Taylor (11)	116
Meike Sanci (11)	117
Kaleel Hassain (13)	118
Filip Bari (11)	119
Darin Mariwan (13)	120
Aiden Carr (12)	121

Green Oak Academy, Moseley

Wanisa Wajid (11)	122
Sidrah Irshad (12)	123
Amal Jama (11)	124
Amina Chowdhury (12)	125
Amina Bilal (11)	126
Yasmin Begum (11)	127
Aleena Rehman (11)	128
Safiyya Ali (11)	129

Oaklands Catholic School & Sixth Form College, Waterlooville

Mathew Justin (12)	130
Jeswin Jaison (12)	131

St Joan Of Arc Catholic School, Rickmansworth

Emilie Tredgold (11)	132
Senuli Godakandaarachchi (11)	133

The Heights Free School, Blackburn

Riley Dixon (13)	134
Kyle Cooper (14)	135
Corey Marsden (14)	136
Mieka Whiteside (14)	137

William Perkin CE High School, Greenford

Suhailah Parvez (13) — 138
Arina Imyanitova (12) — 139
Weronika Stanisz (14) — 140

THE POEMS

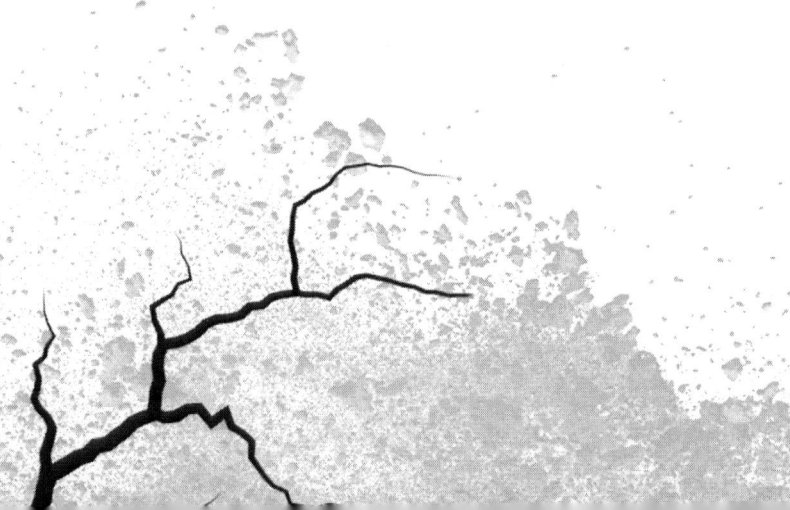

Our Love

I loved her so much, but life goes on,
It was a shame that sadly, she had passed on.
Her looks, her ways, her personality, her smile,
The gorgeous look on her face right before she died.
It tortures, it heartbreaks, it kills, it dreads,
Waiting in the hospital beside her bed.
Cancer is awful, something you shouldn't have to go through,
The look on my face after stage two.
So here I am telling you this poem,
Cancer has no cure, but it doesn't stop you loving.

Charlie-Philip Spencer (11)
Archbishop Sentamu Academy, Hull

Hull United

I play for Hull United
Scored a hat-trick, got me excited
Shouldn't be played in the blistering sun
To play in the raining wet, it's so much fun.

Rugby's always a laugh
They all say, "You'll get hurt"
I laugh, "That's naff."

I play centre mid
I can find a pass like I'm Bruno (Fernandes)
The best at it
You already know.

Drew Hayes (11)
Archbishop Sentamu Academy, Hull

Alton Towers

As I walk through the gates,
Screaming and laughing,
Filled the atmosphere,
Alton Towers is the best place.

Ice-cold drinks,
And warm foods,
The smell runs through my body,
Alton Towers is the best place.

The queues squashed me,
We were like a tin of sardines,
But when I sat in the seat,
I couldn't feel my feet,
Alton Towers is the best place.

Phoebe Holmes (11)
Archbishop Sentamu Academy, Hull

What Is The Best Sport?

F ootball is my favourite sport
O ther sports are good but just not for me
O ver sixty minutes of sport-filled fun
T he best sport for me
B ackline in defence is where I play
A chievements are earned all the time because everyone loves a big trophy
L augh, live and love when playing this game
L ook around, everyone can play football.

Dylan Burke-McGlone (12)
Archbishop Sentamu Academy, Hull

Hull Fair

Hull Fair is a tremendous place to go if you want fear or if you're fearless.
It has very good food, not just sweets
Hot dogs, noodles, toffee apples are my favourite.
It has flashing rides, music and drinks.
If you go and play hook a duck, you will get awesome presents
But don't forget about the bumper cars.
My favourite ride is the waltzer
How about you?

Henley Whalen (11)
Archbishop Sentamu Academy, Hull

Without You

Roses are red
Violets are blue
You're an eight
And I'm a two
Even though people look at you
Not as much as I do
When I saw you, from that day
I knew that I would have to stay.

Roses are red
Violets are blue
My heart is the one for you
I wish we had more time alone
At least I know you're not a clone.

Maisie Briggs (11)
Archbishop Sentamu Academy, Hull

The World Environment

The seas are getting low,
Clouds are going grey,
We need to take control,
So kids can go and play.

The ice is melting,
There's nothing we can do,
Unless we stop global warming,
There will be no reforming.

Now the trees are falling,
Animals are losing their habitats,
Nowhere to go,
They'll die slow.

Adam McCracken (12)
Archbishop Sentamu Academy, Hull

Hull Kingston Rovers

Hull Kingston Rovers are the best team ever.
When you're at the stadium,
You can hear the loudest chants,
Especially the songs.

You need to try the food,
You can have the best, toasty warm food
With ice-cold drinks,
We have all sorts.
I would also be prepared as sardines in the queues,
Also, the stands, check them out.

Paighton Potter-McDaid (11)
Archbishop Sentamu Academy, Hull

The Life Of Rugby

On a cold, wintery day,
The team start to train.
Time ticks down till kick-off.
They get in for a mass game ritual
Rugby is the sport for me.
As the sprinkling rain falls to the ground
The game makes way.
As they slide into the corner
They brush against the grass.
The whistle blows,
Everyone gets cosy inside.

Ellis Fewlass (11)
Archbishop Sentamu Academy, Hull

Football

F ootball is a great sport,
O n the cold, hard ground,
O r on the hot, dead grass,
T o score is hard but I still try,
B e confident with the ball,
A lways a right winger,
L onger pitch every year like your bones,
L ooking like a star when I go through cones.

Natans Peips (12)
Archbishop Sentamu Academy, Hull

Hull Fair

Hull Fair is a great place for everyone.
You can't tell me otherwise.
Hull Fair is the best fair around.
It brings joy and happiness to kids, even parents.
It is a great place for entertainment.
There are loads of sweets, foods and drinks to choose from
And I will assure you, you will have a good night.

Kai Walton (11)
Archbishop Sentamu Academy, Hull

Sports

Rugby, a sport that you would like
One through thirteen, you're in the starting
Fourteen through seventeen, you're on the bench
I thought I would get hurt
Well, rugby's only for me
Prime, water or the power of all drinks
The energy power
Hull FC
Hull KR have their rivalry.

Jaden Harrison (11)
Archbishop Sentamu Academy, Hull

Halloween

Halloween
The queen of mean
The king of sweets
There are so many
Trick-or-treaters.

What a time of year it will be
Little boys and girls dress up
In scary, spooky costumes
Super duper candy on the way home
Halloween
The best night of the year.

Laceymarie Matthews (11)
Archbishop Sentamu Academy, Hull

The Joy Of Pasta

Pasta cannot be beaten,
You also can't convince me enough,
It's got too many types,
That's why,
Pasta cannot be beaten!

People say,
"Pasta is too dry,"
Then get sauces!
If you do that,
Pasta cannot be beaten!

Arminas Stankevičius (11)
Archbishop Sentamu Academy, Hull

Sports

S ports are the best way to have fun outside
P lenty of them to choose
O h, which one, I can't decide
R eally, it will knock off your shoes
T here is tennis, rugby, football and cricket
S o, what are you gonna do?

Lennon Shipley (12)
Archbishop Sentamu Academy, Hull

Be Kind To Nature

Nature is everywhere,
We love nature,
But we are slowly killing it,
God put it in our hands,
It was meant to be treated like a plant,
He wanted us to take care of it until we no longer can,
Stop!
Stop!
The Earth is the best present ever!

Corey Bolton (12)
Archbishop Sentamu Academy, Hull

War Reality

The soldiers are trying to hold back tears
But they are filled with fears.
As the soldiers shoot their guns
They are not having fun.
As they fire
Others are surrounded by barbed wire.
As the soldiers lie
They will die that day.

Ryan Foster (11)
Archbishop Sentamu Academy, Hull

Hull Fair

Hull Fair is my favourite time of the year
It can't be beaten in my eyes
Have you been to Hull Fair?
I have, so let's get to the point
There is candyfloss, hot dogs and burgers
And amazing rides
So you can't miss it.

Eddie Robshaw (11)
Archbishop Sentamu Academy, Hull

Football Day

A slight breeze was just right as I entered the football match.
Football is so fun.
After the match,
I headed home and ate broccoli, chicken and pasta, yum!
After, I was tired so I went to bed.
Another day awaits.

Alfie Thundercliffe (11)
Archbishop Sentamu Academy, Hull

Rugby

Feel the breeze on your face
While you run like you never ran before
Feel the connection of shoulders and legs
See the joy when you win
See the lesson when you lose.

Jamie Hall (12)
Archbishop Sentamu Academy, Hull

Rugby

Rugby should be played
In the rain or cold weather,
To score is hard,
The pitch gets longer every year.

Caiden Penney (11)
Archbishop Sentamu Academy, Hull

We Could Be Destroying The World, We Just Can't See It

We could be destroying the world, we just can't see it,
You're too busy talking on Snapchat,
About how your iPhone 4 is just a piece of tat,
It's the bigger picture that we're not seeing,
Because of climate change, people are running away, fleeing.

Everyone is busy complaining about how things are more expensive,
Or how someone doesn't like something and you find that offensive,
They may be problems but they are small,
Compared to that, climate change is ten feet tall.

We're all talking about how our car has a dent,
Or about the holiday on which we just went,
We need to spend time saving the Earth,
Not wondering how much money you're worth.

If we don't help now, the world will disappear,
This is the message that you need to hear,
We need to save it and we need to save it now,
Start by not eating meat like the cow.

There are many, many things still to do,
Before climate change takes us too,
Global warming is here, you're just too blind to see,
Think about that next time you look at a tree,
We are destroying the world, we just can't see it.

Rachel Cooper (12)
Cyfarthfa High School, Merthyr Tydfil

Change

The newest things are the deadliest things.
The future is coming and darkness is growing,
When you turn a light off the darkness grows.
When you fall asleep and fall,
You suddenly wake up.
Ink grows with pen and water becomes bigger as it spreads.
Wars around the corner, black, white and grey growing.
Great weather leaving,
The green going brown, then grey.
Autumn is around the corner where everything goes brown,
Then when December comes they all go grey.

You would have thought that the snowy times are nice,
Tides push you out but they then pull you in,
Why wouldn't this work for the Arctic?
The jolly times no more,
You think it is better but it is an eco-disaster.
When the diseases break from their icy homes and sea levels flood,
Up, up and up.
The world is melting and our brains explode,
The future may be bad,
But new things are not always that bad.
They are both sad and bad.

The future of the land of the dragon, sheep, and God may be England very soon,
From one rugby nation to a football one.

Freddie Davies (11)
Cyfarthfa High School, Merthyr Tydfil

You Are Not Alone. I'm Hurting Too

Everything is going to be okay, they say.
It will... just as long as you stay strong,
Find support and stand tall, then find a way...
"No one gets how I'm feeling!" is what you may think.
But that's not true because I'm hurting too.
I may know how you feel, it's terrible, isn't it?
The depression, stress, frustration,
Anger, sadness and the pain?
And you may only have a little bit of hope left.
But you need to fight for what you believe in...
Tell them how you really feel, say...
"Let's make a deal!"
You should not feel like this, you don't deserve this.
Love yourself.
Be who you are.
Whether you're drowning in a sea of sadness,
Or if you're a beautiful daisy who is facing their depression,
Or maybe even you are in a field of frustration
And you are lost on where to go.
If you ever feel sad or worried,
Just remember you can win against your feelings!
Throw them in the bin!
You can win... throw them in the bin!

Faith Ison (13)
Cyfarthfa High School, Merthyr Tydfil

Our World

Our world. Our planet. Our environment.
The reason I'm saying this
Is because our world is falling apart.
Pollution, deforestation, global warming,
Wildfires, rubbish everywhere!
The only reason this is happening is because of us!
We need to save our world!
It's getting destroyed because of us.

Throughout my whole life,
I have always seen rubbish just thrown on the floor,
We need to be considerate people
And try to stop throwing rubbish,
At least find a bin or put it in your pocket
Or your bag until you find one.
Our wildlife and sea life are dying
Because of how much pollution and rubbish is everywhere.
We need to save our world.

The poor animals who live on ice are going to die very soon
Because of the ice melting and cracking.
Eventually, we are going to die
And if we don't sort out our world we will destroy our planet.
We need to save the world.

Emilie Halloway (12)
Cyfarthfa High School, Merthyr Tydfil

Quarantine: The Year Of The Wild

Silent are the streets, still lie the malls
Locked in a house with the world behind walls
For the year of the wild is no human feat
As in the wake of their absence, birds sing and tweet
Animals roam, unbound from their shackles
Yet as the year comes to an end, humanity cackles
They brandish their arms, aglow in their home
The wild unaware of the doom to unfold
"Covid is gone!" the reporters boom
Hunters stand ready, prepared to cause doom
Thick, black clouds envelop the roads
Cars whizzing by and polluting their home
Animals lie, asleep in the mud
When gunshots ring out with a monstrous thud
Species die out, habitats fall
The world starts to burn; for what cause was this all?
A hunter sits on a couch, looking awfully smug
Next to the fireplace lies a bear-skin rug.

Logan Jenkins (12)
Cyfarthfa High School, Merthyr Tydfil

Normal

Just because you're walking down the street and see two women kissing doesn't mean you have to point it out.
If you were walking down the street and saw two men together it doesn't mean they're gay.
Because if you were in the car and looked out the window and saw a man and a woman you wouldn't say anything because it's 'normal'.
But what is normal?
Is it being straight, gay or lesbian?
No, 'normal' is just a word!
Not one person on this Earth is 'normal'!
Everyone is different, no one is perfect and that's why you shouldn't judge people.
What if being part of the LGBTQ was 'normal' and being straight was 'different', people staring at you every time you walk down the street?
Everyone is different, there is no such thing as 'normal'!

Maddie Moule (12)
Cyfarthfa High School, Merthyr Tydfil

The Environment, Our World

Stop!
Make a difference,
Don't throw your rubbish on the floor,
Put it in a bin where it belongs.
Hunting animals?
They're getting extinct,
Some animals we need in this world to survive.
Why use so much water and waste it?
There are people in the world who don't have as much.

Why?
Why are you cutting down the trees?
They are very, very important in this world, not phones.
We need trees to live.
Climate change.
There is more rain going on in one part of the world and more heat in another
The climate is changing and more disasters could happen!

We need your help.
I'm saying this because our world is falling apart,
It's breaking, it's dying,
And if we don't do anything about it,
We're going to die with the world!

Nancy Gordon (11)
Cyfarthfa High School, Merthyr Tydfil

Racism In Sport

Racism is a big thing in sport
No human should have to put up with it
If your child uses racist words
Then your child needs to be taught!

Bullying is bad enough
Kids and adults are being treated wrong
And what they're going through
It's tough!

Two years ago in a worldwide game
Three players missed a pen
Rashford, Sancho and Saka
Were their given names!

England was one step away from winning
It was a tough game, we could all tell from the beginning!
After the match, all you would read online would be
'How could you miss that, you ugly- '.

Being hurt because of their skin
Why don't you keep your dirty, nasty mouth
In the bin!

Olivia Atherton
Cyfarthfa High School, Merthyr Tydfil

Women Of Iran

Haiku poetry

Women of Iran
Why are they being oppressed?
Hijabs are a choice.

Women of Iran
Why are they being killed there?
Freedom is a right.

Women of Iran
Why are they burning hijabs?
What is going on?

Police, why, just why?
You should be protecting them
Not attacking them.

Who are we to judge?
To be judging what they wear
It is their bodies.

Fire lights the night
Women are dancing around
"Down with hijab rules!"

Iran policemen
Help the women of Iran
They really need it.

Hijab is a choice
We need to make it just theirs
Women of Iran.

Katie James (12)
Cyfarthfa High School, Merthyr Tydfil

Pollution

Factory smoke paints the sky,
Misty grey is all that can be seen,
The sun is engulfed by sad smoke,
Peculiar pollution, in the night sky.

Shadows of people are disguised
As more smoke in the sky,
Colourless life is everywhere to be seen,
Peculiar pollution rots the water.

The local rivers and lakes are blanketed
In plastic waste,
The old home for the fish is now
Nothing more than a rubbish bin,
Peculiar pollution takes over the town.

An eerie feeling lingers on the street
As people go to sleep,
Once green grass is now replaced by greenhouse gases,
Peculiar pollution destroys the Earth.

Darcie Edwards (12)
Cyfarthfa High School, Merthyr Tydfil

Let Me Sleep

The sunlight disturbs my slumber,
But my blanket encourages me to go back to sleep.
My mother acts like an alarm clock,
But I block out the noise by burying my face.
Clothes are placed at the end of my bed,
But I ignore them because I am comfortable.
The rest of the house is moving - brothers making noise,
I realise that I am losing the battle and that my sleep has been destroyed.
Miserable, I admit my defeat and leave my lair,
Counting the moments until I can go back to sleep.
In the car I whine and groan,
Wanting to go back home.
We're now at school and the day has begun,
Battle is over - the sunlight has won.

Isabella Phillips (11)
Cyfarthfa High School, Merthyr Tydfil

Help The Ocean

1.3 billion plastic bottles are used each day
And that's forty billion in one month
And that's an extremely large amount
And most of them don't end up being reused
And just end up going to waste in the ocean.

We need to stop ocean pollution for several reasons
Like if we don't act fast, sea turtles will go extinct.

Years ago we thought we would be fine but we're not
And if we keep this up and don't realise what we are all doing
Our planet could be destroyed.

So please recycle your plastics
Put your plastic in the bin
And together we will win
And stop ocean pollution.

Evan Walker (11)
Cyfarthfa High School, Merthyr Tydfil

Nobody Knows Me Better

Today I found a friend who knew everything
I felt she knew my weaknesses and the problems I've been dealt
She understood my wonders and listened to my dreams
She listened to how I felt about life and love and knew what it all meant
Not once did she interrupt me or tell me that I was wrong
She understood what I was going through
And promised me she would stay all the time
I reached out to this friend to show her that I care
To pull her close and let her know how much I needed her there
I went to hold her hand, to pull her a bit nearer
And realised that this perfect friend I found was nothing, just my mirror.

Scarlett James (11)
Cyfarthfa High School, Merthyr Tydfil

Testing On Animals

Why is it that between seventeen and thirty-two million animals get tested on each year?
Why is it that between sixteen and twenty million animals get tested on each month?
Why is it that between eight and twelve million animals get tested on each week?
Why is it that between two and six million animals get tested on each day?
Governments blinded by their stacks of cash,
Not realising that animals are getting forced into this madness.
The animals getting strapped down,
Not realising what's about to happen,
Needles stuck in them.
No one realises this torture happens,
No one realises that this needs to stop.

Samuel Cole (11)
Cyfarthfa High School, Merthyr Tydfil

Back In 2020

It all started in March 2020
When we were all put into lockdown
It was only meant to be two weeks
But ended up lasting for two years.

We were all stuck in our houses
With no education, nothing
Covid tests were everywhere
In-store, online, everywhere you looked.

Over one thousand people died during Covid
Many still in hospital, sick and dying
Lots lost their family members
Many missed out on their school education.

Still to this day, it's still around
But at least we aren't in lockdown
People still take precautions
While another jab is still in motion.

Summer Simons (13)
Cyfarthfa High School, Merthyr Tydfil

Plastic

Plastic is bad
Plastic is sad
No more plastic bags
No more plastic straws
Don't be using fifteen million pieces of plastic every year
That's too much
Paper, I said paper, stop
Two million trees get cut down every day
That's too much
That's bad
This makes me mad
Now the ocean and the sea
Has 269,000 tons of rubbish every day
How can this be?
This is bad
This makes me mad
Food waste in the UK
We waste 6.7 million tons per year
This costs £10.2 billion
This is mad
So, so sad
Think, reduce, reuse, recycle.

Jake Williams (11)
Cyfarthfa High School, Merthyr Tydfil

Our Lives In Covid

It was a terrible time in our lives
We were all kept in with kids, husbands and wives
People lost family members
Some children didn't go to school till September.

The sun was very bright
The room in hospitals was very tight
Home learning was hard
Many children missed out because they were barred.

Toilet roll was all the rage
But then the jab was made
Lots of shops shut
Even Pizza Hut.

If you cough, take a test
If you don't, people will pester
Will it go back to how it was before?
Or will it be like this forevermore?

Olivia Jones (12)
Cyfarthfa High School, Merthyr Tydfil

Careless Damages

We pollute the planet
We damage the planet
We hurt the planet
Yet we don't care.

We pollute the oceans
We damage the oceans
We hurt the oceans
Yet we don't care.

We pollute the land
We damage the land
We hurt the land
Yet we don't care.

We hurt the animals
We kill the animals
We eat the animals
Yet we don't care.

We kill
We hurt
We pollute
We damage
Yet we don't care.

But we should
Let's save the Earth
While we can, before it's too late.

Nasko Ognyanov (12)
Cyfarthfa High School, Merthyr Tydfil

The Cost Of Paper

Paper, I said paper.
Paper is made of wood and trees.
Over two million trees are cut down every day.
We need trees to breathe, to stay alive.
And every second a football pitch is covered by trees.
But there is stone paper, however, it's twenty-seven pounds.
We are in a time of a cost of living crisis.
We pay to stay alive.
And we might not live anymore
Because of trees being cut down.
So I, Macsen James Wiliams, *urge* companies
To *stop* cutting trees down and make stone paper cheaper.
Let's make change for the greater good.

Macsen Williams (11)
Cyfarthfa High School, Merthyr Tydfil

My Family

So here is a poem written by me,
About the rest of my amazing family.
First, there is my mam, her name is Lucy,
She works in a school as well you see.
Then there's me dad, he's a folder operator,
But his real art is as a master smell creator.
Next, we have my little brother, his name is Iwan,
He's lots of fun to play with and is the funniest human.
Last but not least is our loyal dog named Drake,
There's nothing he likes better than a hot and juicy steak.
So that's my amazing and special family,
They all mean a great deal to me.

Caitlin Davies
Cyfarthfa High School, Merthyr Tydfil

Queen Elizabeth

A dedicated monarch for seventy years
A young girl being crowned
She showed the crowd that she had what it took to make them proud.

In the end, she was laid to rest
With full pomp and ceremony like Britain does best.

Her pony and corgis were there to say goodbye
With a nation in tears and her family standing proud.

Her son is now king
To carry on the great service she did for Great Britain and the Commonwealth
We all say God bless and rest up above
With your husband Philip and your mam and dad.

Oliver Powell (11)
Cyfarthfa High School, Merthyr Tydfil

Save The Sea Animals

The sea animals are dying
Because of the plastic in the ocean
Just chilling, eating plastic on a daily basis
The plastic in the ocean is everyone's fault
Recycle your plastic and we could have fun
The sea animals would not be hurt anymore
So use reusable plastics
And the sea animals will not be hurt anymore
Recycling could save many animals' lives
So recycle your plastics and we will have far fewer problems
So we need to save the beautiful sea animals
For the future generations that are above us all.

Chloe Gordon (13)
Cyfarthfa High School, Merthyr Tydfil

Bullying

     B e kind to other people
yo **U** want respect? You've got to give it.
     L ying about people won't get you far in life.
     L earn to respect the rules and other people.
     Y es, sometimes people will be rude to you, but don't retaliate.
     I n primary, I was bullied and it was the worst thing ever!
     N o, just because they hit first doesn't mean you can hit back.
     G etting bullied is the worst feeling ever, so please don't put anyone through it.

Jacob Burton (13)
Cyfarthfa High School, Merthyr Tydfil

The Signs

The tweeting of birds,
The chatting of friends,
Yet there were never any meetings to attend.

The scrolling through apps,
The images being sent,
Though with the liking and sharing,
Was it truly meant?

Being 'on call' for hours at a time,
With just filters and dancing,
No song, no rhyme.

The sound of crying and pressure and pain,
These are the signs of cyberbullying,
And once it's gone,
It'll come back again.

Jessica Craze (14)
Cyfarthfa High School, Merthyr Tydfil

If I Had A Magic Wand

If I had a magic wand, I would wave it every day.
I would wish and wave all suffering away.
I would stop all war and heal the sick and take all pain away.

Oh, but if I had a magic wand, I would use it every day.
I would feed the world, there would be no drought.
The plants would grow, the leaves would sprout.
The fruit would grow, the crops would yield.
Then no matter what, the world would heal!

Oh, if I had a magic wand, I would wave it every day.

Chloe Harding (11)
Cyfarthfa High School, Merthyr Tydfil

Pity

Soaking in my own disgust
I stared into her eyes as I melted
Swallowed in pity I gifted myself
I looked at my childhood
A warm evening, mid-June
I twist her hair around my finger
And plant a kiss on her forehead
Sorrowful tears flowing down my cheek
As I cradle her in my arms
Like a mother would
Wiping the damp, sticky hair
Off her forehead
Damping her pink, cotton shirt with my pitiful tears
I fear I may never see her like that again.

Olivia Kaczynska (14)
Cyfarthfa High School, Merthyr Tydfil

What Is War?

War is a vast abyss.
Once it starts it never stops,
War is a never-ending cycle.
Nobody wins or loses in the end.

War does not only hurt us but our planet as well.
The bombs, planes and gunshots add to the pollution,
War kills, hurts and injures.
Thousands of injured and killed for nothing in the end.

Wars have no true meaning.
Just governments wanting more land to wreck.
War is pointless.
So why do we do it?
Just to kill?

Skye Lewis (12)
Cyfarthfa High School, Merthyr Tydfil

Equality Between Us

Men and women are the same
Here equality is my aim
White, black or mixed race
Don't judge, let them go at their own pace.

From your sister to your brother
To your father and your mother
Love your family, friends and teachers
Your neighbours, priests and preachers.

Don't judge a book by its cover
Always think, take care of each other
Be the best you, you can be.

Equality between us counts
Don't you agree?

Lily-Beth McGovern (12)
Cyfarthfa High School, Merthyr Tydfil

Why?

Why do men and women,
Both being cheated by the government,
Have to hate each other so much?
And why do so many races,
Walking the poverty line like a tightrope,
Have to be at each other's throats every day?
And why does the 'more intelligent' species
Have to keep the others in cages?
Why?
Why do we hate, when we have the power to create?
Why do we use our minds to destroy?
How are we so blind to the pain we cause?
Why?

Josh Billingsley (11)
Cyfarthfa High School, Merthyr Tydfil

Let The Stars Shimmer

You lie awake in the midst of night
Light floods through your window; the city alight
You stare past the window
And into the stars
But the shimmering stars that once covered the sky
Were little in number and beginning to die
For every light at night turned on
Another gorgeous star is gone
But by turning off the lights
Another star takes flight
To save the stars, it's the only solution
Turn off your lights to halt light pollution.

Ethan Jenkins (12)
Cyfarthfa High School, Merthyr Tydfil

Black Holes

Predicted by Einstein's theory,
Studied by Hawking the prof,
They form from the violent death of a star.
Black holes are not the empty space you think they are,
Nothing, not even light can escape,
Though in the quantum world this may not be the case.
If you come across one and fall into the black,
Are you lost forever, never coming back?
Or are you spat out of a hole that is white,
Into another place in space and time?

George Davies (11)
Cyfarthfa High School, Merthyr Tydfil

Bullying Is Bad

Why are some bullied while others are not?
Why do people hurt others?
Why do people cry themselves to sleep?
Bullying is why.
Do bullies do it for the fun of it?
Nobody knows.
People can be bullied for anything.
Their hair, the way they act or even their skin.
Students ignore it when they should be stopping it!
Even talking to a teacher or parent can make a difference!
Stop bullying!

Ellie Pearce (11)
Cyfarthfa High School, Merthyr Tydfil

Bully

I hate the way you kick and punch
I hate the way you steal people's lunch
I hate the way you always stare
I hate the way you always swear
I hate the way you always tell
I hate the way you always make my life a living hell
I hate the way you think you're so strong
I hate the way you think I'm wrong
I hate the way you never stop
But one day you will be in for a shock.

Emily Sullivan (11)
Cyfarthfa High School, Merthyr Tydfil

The Man On The Street

Homelessness is hard,
People suffer on the street,
I was rejected.

People stare at me,
On the street, it's so cold,
I feel very useless.

They say, "Good morning,"
They don't really care about me,
They care about themselves.

I feel dejected,
I wish they could live like me,
"Please help me," I say.

Will Mackie (13)
Cyfarthfa High School, Merthyr Tydfil

War Grows Near

Black mist fills the air with worry and confusion
Buildings lie damaged and deserted
Streets stay empty and unwanted
Unsettling noises go off in the distance
Everybody wonders what the screams and cries a few miles away mean
Children learn things that no one can explain
Families struggle to live another day
People don't know what to stay.

Emilia Jones (11)
Cyfarthfa High School, Merthyr Tydfil

Racism

Red dog, blue dog, pink dog or yellow dog,
No matter the colour we are all a dog,
This dog owns a car, this dog owns a bar,
This dog lives afar, but we are all still a dog,
This one likes painting, this one likes drawing,
Still, it doesn't matter what you look like,
Your colour, what you own or what you like,
You are still just a dog.

Dylan Hughes (12)
Cyfarthfa High School, Merthyr Tydfil

Imagine

Imagine being scared of your friends.
Imagine having to hide from a gunman.
Imagine your teachers carrying a gun.
Imagine families when their children don't come home.
Imagine wanting to kill innocent children.
Imagine, just imagine,
A normal day turning into a life-threatening day.

Addison Pulman (11)
Cyfarthfa High School, Merthyr Tydfil

Two Weeks In 2020

L oneliness at home
O utbreak is happening
C ovid cases are rising
K nowing people are at risk
D eaths from Covid
O n our own, day in, day out
W orrying about your family and friends
N ot knowing when we will see family and friends.

Reese Gray (12)
Cyfarthfa High School, Merthyr Tydfil

Schizophrenia

I wake and see it...
The man in the corner is staring at me again
I scream and shout, trying to escape
This everlasting nightmare...
I throw and toss objects at it but nothing works
But then I see nothing is there
The man is gone
My nightmare is over.

Lucas O'Neill (12)
Cyfarthfa High School, Merthyr Tydfil

Wales

W ales is known as the 'Land of Song'
A ncient history and charming language
L eeks and daffodils are worn with pride
E isteddfod is a Welsh celebration
S t David is the patron saint of Wales.

Alfie Williams (11)
Cyfarthfa High School, Merthyr Tydfil

It's Time To Act!

When I look around, I see the world surrounding me.
When I look around, I see trees of green and skies of bright blue.
When I look around, I see smiles of superb joy on people's faces.
Yet, something isn't right.

The ocean is being polluted like tons of marbles being spilt upon the floor.
The trees are being cut down in a matter of seconds.
Our Earth is experiencing climate change and we have currently done nothing about it.
So what are you waiting for?
This is our future!
It's our responsibility to change it!

So what do we do, you may ask?
Stop using plastic products.
Recycle and reuse.
Commit to quitting toxic fuels.
But most importantly, spread the word.
Let them know what you think.
Tell them all you've heard because this is your world to sync.
This is your future.
And it's changing in seconds.
Changing as fast as the blink of an eye.

So take a glance around you.
Look deeper into the surface to truly break through.
Maybe then, you'll see the gases and fuels being released into the air.
Maybe then, you'll see the amounts of plastic being released into the seas.
Maybe then, you'll see the polluted planet that generations of people have created over time.

But don't worry, this won't be our future;
We shall change it.

Susie Wasielewska (12)
Excelsior Academy, Newcastle Upon Tyne

Money

Earth is crumbling
Inequality is growing
Money's true colours are showing
Hope is pouring
What would we do without even knowing?
This is definitely the government's doing
All it deserves is some big, fat booing
You don't know what you're talking about
This is just money, and all the suing
Money, you're right
Money, money, money
Ain't it funny?
Living in such a world
That values money more than literally anything
What does it even bring?
It's just some paper and a coin
With the same metal material as my silver ring
Money, money, money
We call it 'fair'
Taxes, paper, coins
But in return we get some wooden chair
Money, money, money
It's real funny
How some have none
But lots have a ton

And it still falls under the name 'fair'?
Oh money, money, money
Climate change, pollution
All because of money
Yea, that's the real enemy here
Our planet's value is way more than some papers and coins
Get that into your head
Start working and seriously get up from that bed
Money, money, money
It's real funny.

Yasmeen Khalaf (11)
Excelsior Academy, Newcastle Upon Tyne

Time Just Goes By

Get up from bed
Get ready to go to school
Time goes by
Then I am late.

Time goes by
Got detention for being rude
Saying sorry does not work.

Time goes by
Starting to get angrier and angrier
Stroking my nose in anger relaxes me.

Time goes by
It's the end of the day
Getting sleepy
Going to bed to sleep.

Now on another day
Everything repeats itself
Get up from bed
Get ready to go to school
Time goes by
This time not late.

Time goes by
I am focused
I am brave

Get points after points
Learning and learning.

Time goes by
It's the end of the day
Go to sleep
Eight hours straight.

It's another day
The day where it's the start of Black History Month
Go to school
Not late
Time goes by.

There is something feeling strange
No teachers are talking about Black History
Tell them about it
They're shocked
No one seemed to remember.

Time goes by
No one seemed to care
The only thing I was thinking about
Was getting out of there.

Rejoice Akenvwa (12)
Excelsior Academy, Newcastle Upon Tyne

Climate Change

I wrote this poem because of climate change
I hope that everyone who reads this will join me in helping.

It's just sad because every time I go to the beach
I just see the dead animals
Like baby crabs and dead baby fish
It's because they choke on the plastic that's in the sea.

There are kids, adults
They are all starving
We need more help
We need to get up and be brave.

I know the world is a dangerous place
But do you know why it's dangerous?
It's because we made it dangerous
Because no one is helping
And I can't believe that there are millions of people starving
But we can change this.

Do you know how we can change this?
If we all get up and help
And if we do help all the animals
We would be happy
And all of the kids would be happy as well
And the world would not be dangerous.

And if everyone is happy
The world would be fantastic
I hope that everyone sees this
And that they will change their minds
And I hope they change it for the better
And I hope everyone has a nice day.

Erfan Jadari (11)
Excelsior Academy, Newcastle Upon Tyne

Enough Is Enough!

Racism is a big thing in society and it needs to stop,
It's been going on for ages and we need to make a change;
In 2020 when George Floyd was killed,
No one helped him, no one said a thing.
Skin colour doesn't determine if you're a criminal or not.
The hatred towards coloured people has gone on long enough.

We are getting abused over something we can't control.
Getting called the N-word, P-word, C-word, terrorist.
The list goes on.
Used to be sold like we weren't humans.
Forced into labour and outcast into the ghetto for being Jewish.
Like, why does it make a difference if I believe in what I want?

One terrorist attack and billions of people get blamed.
What did we have to do with that?
Getting called letter boxes for wearing something I choose to wear.
No, I am not oppressed or forced!
My beliefs do not affect you.

Leave us alone, that's all we ever asked.
We want our justice and peace.

It's been going on ever since our ancestors were born.
Enough is enough!

Nusrat Karim (14)
Excelsior Academy, Newcastle Upon Tyne

Equality

Equality,
It's something we should all have, isn't it?
So why do people have to fight?
To work for basic human rights?
Why are they shamed?
Because of their gender, their sexuality, their race?
Black people are being killed by police brutality,
Women don't feel safe walking down the street,
Homophobic hate crimes tripled last year alone,
Why do we condone all the people who are scared of what they do not know?

Equality,
It's something we should all have,
So why don't we?
Because of the people who don't seem to realise,
That we do not want to compromise for our rights,
We need to treat everyone equally,
We need to give everyone an opportunity to show us who they are without stereotypes getting in the way,
Without how they look getting in the way,
Without who they love getting in the way.

Danielle Faichen (13)
Excelsior Academy, Newcastle Upon Tyne

Bullying

Bullying is wrong
Bullying can end lives
Bullying makes people depressed
Bullying makes people lonely
Bullying needs to end
Bullying can be hurtful
Bullying online is worse inside
Bullying is abusive
Bullying can cause destruction for people
Bullying is the worst thing for a person to suffer
Bullying makes people cry
Bullying makes people suicidal
Bullying makes people quiet
Bullying is not a good thing
Bullying can lead to them becoming a bully
Bullying will make people think that they are not a good person
Bullying might make people hate themselves
Bullying could make people feel wrong about themselves
Bullying could make people sad and fake being okay.

James Dixon (12)
Excelsior Academy, Newcastle Upon Tyne

It Is Your Choice

The sun is yellow,
The sun is burning the Earth,
Like burning your hand,
We all know Mercury,
One day that will be us,
Too hot to survive,
Too toxic to survive,
We only have one Earth,
Our Earth is not a meal that is waiting there,
Do not hurt our home,
Because when we need it most,
It won't be there,
So why hurt our home?
How much will it take?
How much will it take to realise,
That it is not too late,
Never too late to help?
When a teacher helps you,
You be that teacher,
Do it for the Earth,
Do it for our home,
Be that teacher to help the Earth,
Be that person who makes a difference,
Repay the favour,
The Earth gave you a home,

So make the Earth feel like a home,
Because one day the Earth won't be there,
It is your choice.

Summer Rose Forster (13)
Excelsior Academy, Newcastle Upon Tyne

Your Inspiration

How are you inspired?
Are you inspired by the sun?
Does it warm your skin from deep within?
Is it your number one?

Is it the pounding rain that makes you want to write?
When you hear the plop of the first few drops is it
something you can't fight?

Or does it take heartache?
A pain that runs so deep.
A mournful cry that made you sigh for the secrets you kept?

Are you inspired by sorrow?
The wretched, lonely ache of a lonely soul that has no goal?
Is this what it will take?

Do you look for inspiration or does it look for you?
Will it be your friend until the end?
Tell me what inspires you.

Melissa Milova (12)
Excelsior Academy, Newcastle Upon Tyne

Bullying

Why is it that bullying happens?
Why is it that people think it's okay?
Why is it that bullying happens?
A bullied heart is a broken heart
Defenceless bodies of innocent kids get bullied every day
Physical abuse is hurting poor teenagers
Mental abuse is chipping away at people's mental health and self-esteem
The scars you can't see sometimes hurt the most
Innocent people with insecure thoughts
Bullying can lead to much worse
And why? Because you get pleasure out of it?
We need to help the people who can't speak up
Before more get hurt
We are the future
We can help
We can stop it all.

Maddison Palmer (11)
Excelsior Academy, Newcastle Upon Tyne

Save The Animals

Now more than ever you are needed.
For our favourite creatures need your help.
From the smallest ant to the biggest elephant
They are losing their homes and their lives.
With their terrified eyes and shaking bodies
They whimper and hide from poachers
Day and night clinging on to life.
Hopefully in the years to come
Saving the animals can be done.
But my one burning question is
Do you need the extra stepping stool or chair?
As it is destroying animals' habitats
And leaving them to die.
Please join me and fight the government
To save our creatures
That the next generation might not see.

Daniel Lowdon (11)
Excelsior Academy, Newcastle Upon Tyne

Mental Health

Mental health is important,
Mental health should be heard,
Everybody has a voice,
Everybody has a reason,
Nobody deserves the pain of depression,
Nobody doesn't need this life lesson,
Men are taught not to cry,
To always be strong,
Even through the night,
Women are taught to be respectable,
Dress respectably and do not be touched,
If they do it's their fault, right?
Mental health is important,
Mental health should be heard,
Why must people be challenged?
Pained?
Why must we hurt?
Suicide,
The killer,
Millions caused daily,
The reason,
Mental health.

Tamara Potter (13)
Excelsior Academy, Newcastle Upon Tyne

All The Stress This World Gives Me

My question to all of you is,
How do you deal with all of the struggles
That you go through every single day,
Without getting the time to express them to anyone?
Am I the only one who feels this way?
Am I the only one who can feel all the pressure?
It's our responsibility to get up every day
And try our best to smile,
But I can't hide it anymore,
All the stress and struggles that we go through need to end.
It's starting to feel harder and harder
To get up out of bed every day,
This is how I feel.
How can we as people
Overcome all the hate and stress we get every day?

Fatima Ethni (12)
Excelsior Academy, Newcastle Upon Tyne

Blinded By Rage

People enjoy the luxuries of life,
Oblivious to the conflict, war and strife.
Leagues away from the terrible truth.
Fight for your country or let it lie,
Awaiting its destruction when they shall die.

The plight of battle, that none should bear.
The awful sight, the death and suffering,
All borne until they rest.
A final breath, to sleep eternal.

Lest we end the appalling fights.
The deaths of millions, killed in battle.
But it doesn't have to be this way.
When they see the light, when they stop the fight,
That is when wrong will be right.

Thenuk Themiya Kodithuwakku (11)
Excelsior Academy, Newcastle Upon Tyne

The News At Seven

Isolation and destruction,
Anger-bait, induction,
Politics, old men's antics,
Foes and fools,
Is all I see when I
Turn on the news.
BBC3, fear for free!
Sky One, you're not alone!
ITV2, there's no hope for you!
Solar flares, pollution,
Men in black ties!
Depression in teens is at an all-time high!
Is there a sign? Is there an end?
Our Earth is dying, it all feels like a lie!
Our Newsround is grim
My hopes are getting dim.
Will anyone ever see heaven?
But that situation's normal for the
News at seven.

Freya Rodmell (11)
Excelsior Academy, Newcastle Upon Tyne

Abandoned

I don't see the point
She keeps saying write down anything
But what?
What is
Anything?
I don't like a blank piece of paper
It stares back at me, challenging me to start.

He stares at the table, grinning through his hand
The boy at the front
Who hopes he's not asked
But all of his hopes will be dashed
He's next
He shifts uncomfortably on his scar
Looking around for solidarity
But he is abandoned by those he hopes will back him
His friends are only glad
It's *not their turn...*
This time.

Richard Pina (13)
Excelsior Academy, Newcastle Upon Tyne

Suicide

Suicide is a real risk
It's something that should not exist
They feel like they're next on the list
They're always clenching their fists.

There must be another way
There should be no need to pray
They've been counting down since the start of May
Harming themselves as if they need to pay.

It's hidden in the air
Pulling out their hair
Twitching in their chair
This used to be rare.

Now this is my speech
I would like you to preach
These things they don't teach
So this is my speech.

Joseph Bowes (13)
Excelsior Academy, Newcastle Upon Tyne

This Is Real, Life Is Not A Video Game

Real life isn't a video game
Most people sit on their bum all day
Wasting their life on a dumb game
I mean get off your Xbox or PlayStation
And get yourself outside
Play football or basketball with your mates
Also you could go to the library or bath to read
I like to read, indeed, with a leed
I used to only play games on PS4
But then I saw this clip on YouTube
Of a little boy who got grounded for a year for playing
So please, please take part in the real world
Not a video game
Only play on weekends
Not all the time.

Aiden Lee Murray (11)
Excelsior Academy, Newcastle Upon Tyne

Find Your Voice

High school people liked that I was happy but people came up to me.
I didn't know at the time that they were insulting me.
They called me names, looked at my body.
I never told anyone 'cause I didn't have a voice.
Sometimes I felt like I didn't want to be here, in life.
It came to the point where I wanted to rip the skin off my body.
But I found my voice in this poem.
I don't want people to have to endure the pain I went through.
Find your voice, make people listen to your story, to your words.
We still have time.

Lauren White (13)
Excelsior Academy, Newcastle Upon Tyne

Cyberbullying

I believe cyberbullying should be classified as a crime
Why would people even waste their time
All cyberbullies we can't trust, they cyberbully just for fun.

Listen and look
Don't cyberbully
Listen and look
Be yourself
Listen and look
For advice.

Step one: Tell an adult or teacher
Step two: Ask them to delete it
Step three: If they don't, tell the adult
Step four: The adult will confront that child
Step five: It's deleted.

Crystabel Agbonwaneten (11)
Excelsior Academy, Newcastle Upon Tyne

Home

Are you okay?
Yes, I am fine
Did you have a good day?
It was okay
Turn your phone down!
I am
Where have you been?
They made me come the long way
Why is it me?
I don't know
Do your homework!
I don't have any
What do you want for tea?
Mozzarella sticks
Go in the bath!
I am, I will run it
Do your work!
What work?
Where is your money?
On the bus
Get upstairs
Okay
Shut the door
Why?

Take your socks off
No, they keep my feet warm.

Miley Humble (12)
Excelsior Academy, Newcastle Upon Tyne

Stop Or It Will Infect The Future

F uel kills, not supplies,
O h, when will the energy companies reply,
S ue people who support fossil fuels,
S top wasting water, use reusable pools,
I 'll write until it stops,
L ife will change pops.

F ear the karma,
U tilise the species that might go,
E liminate the illegal poachers!
L ove them before it's their last day,
S top it now, it is my final cry.

Waqar Rahman (11)
Excelsior Academy, Newcastle Upon Tyne

Don't Kill The Animals On This Planet

Animals, mainly tigers, don't they get to live?
We, the humans, will be the end of them,
60% of animals have faded away,
When will we learn?
When will we see?
For all of us to live we need to save wildlife.

Their homes,tall and small, are getting destroyed,
And their lives follow, not far behind,
The tigers, one of the species we kill,
It has to stop and we have to see,
Killing our animals is not a path I want to see.

Charlie Todd (11)
Excelsior Academy, Newcastle Upon Tyne

Racism

R acism is unacceptable yet it still happens so often.
A t least once a day I hear a racist slur that applies to me as well.
C an we fix this problem?
I think we can!
S o the next time you see some racist activity, are you going to tell them that it's not okay and take a stand?
M y wish is that people go colourblind and don't see the colour of people as a problem, please help my wish come true.

Azlan Zahidi (14)
Excelsior Academy, Newcastle Upon Tyne

It's Just Not Fair

Where's my money?
You don't have any change
Did you have a good day?
Yes, I had fun
Do your homework
I will give it a chance
Go and play out
I am, don't worry
Fold your clothes
Okay, I just walked through the door
Go upstairs and get ready
Okay, I am going now
What do you want for your tea?
I don't care, you choose
Go up to Iceland for me
Okay then, give us some money.

Elisha Waterston (11)
Excelsior Academy, Newcastle Upon Tyne

Problems In The Earth

Many teenagers go around in groups
And often join a gang
They think it's cool to carry guns
That can take a life in just one bang!
They think they are hard
And also very clever
But to use a gun on someone
Will change their lives forever.

Some people will not use a gun
But instead they have a knife
And it takes one dumb move
To take somebody's life forever.

Lives, not knives.

Albaz Mohammed (11)
Excelsior Academy, Newcastle Upon Tyne

I Like And Hate

I like sausages
I like beans
I don't like macaroni and cheese
I like ice cream
I like cake
Especially the ones I make
I like strawberry jolly jam
And buttered toast
I like breakfast food the most
I hate it when people say, "Eww! That's just gross"
I like dollars! I like bills!
I don't like it when people steal
It's not fair
None of my diamond accessories are rare.

Stephanie Chapim (11)
Excelsior Academy, Newcastle Upon Tyne

Earth Is Dying

The Earth is dying and it's from gas
Like planes flying
We should start listening
We're all dying, especially the Earth
We should treat it like a baby
One day it will stop
Just maybe
You are killing the animals screaming in terror
If the animals and plants could speak
They would say, "Never," to climate change
So remember, if the world could speak
It would say, "Never."

Will Sharp (11)
Excelsior Academy, Newcastle Upon Tyne

Stop Littering

L et's stop littering,
I t will help the animals that are dying,
T ake your rubbish to the bin,
T ell your family and friend to stop,
E very time you litter, hundreds of animals are dying,
R ealise now what you have to do,
I f you don't, animals will die more than you expect,
N ot all people are listening to me
G et your feet back on track.

Habiba Sultana (11)
Excelsior Academy, Newcastle Upon Tyne

World Wars

This world is a failure,
Up and down,
Just a planet,
With a lot of sound,
Death after death,
Cry after cry,
Why won't it stop?
Nobody knows why,
People die while people cry,
"It's really hard to stop,"
Say the people who start,
"It's really hard to accept,"
Say the broken souls of loved ones,
It'll never end,
Unfortunately, why?

Damon Graham (11)
Excelsior Academy, Newcastle Upon Tyne

Stop Bullying!

B ullies are not worth it.
U sually they hypnotise you into thinking fake things about you.
L ove yourself, no matter how you look or what you have.
L eave me alone, I just want to shout.
Y ou're perfect, don't change who you are.
I can tell you
N o one deserves to be bullied.
G o stand up for yourself.

Zaima Azad (11)
Excelsior Academy, Newcastle Upon Tyne

It's Just Not Fair

Tidy your room
But I have!
It's so unfair
I always get the blame!
C1, C2, C3, C4
But I did nothing wrong!
You're late
I have a reason!
Stop talking
It is not me!

It makes me feel like a raging bull!

I always get the blame
It's just not fair
I always get C1, C2, C3, C4
People always blame me!

Tia-Faith Ferguson (11)
Excelsior Academy, Newcastle Upon Tyne

Idiots Across The Internet

The internet, everybody reads it.
Some people love it.
Whilst others hate it.
People use it for stupid things.
Others use it to brighten others' days.
Then there are people who hack and scam.
They are filth.
Some people just put up their opinions.
Others disagree.
Then start wars.
In the end quit, ban stupid people.

Kaine Wilkinson (14)
Excelsior Academy, Newcastle Upon Tyne

Just Walk Away

It's a horrible thing,
Called 'bullying',
And people do it with anything and everything.
It'll get you down,
Give you a big, fat frown,
But just walk away,
We can change stuff, now.
Don't bite back and cause drama,
You'll just go back crying to your mama,
Just walk away, I swear, it'll be okay.

Grace Igo (12)
Excelsior Academy, Newcastle Upon Tyne

Death

Death is when your loved ones must depart,
Death is a sharp pain in the heart,
Death is a feeling of permanent sadness and pain,
Death is when your loved ones have forever gone away,
Death is a call to heaven or hell,
Death is an eternal mansion or cell,
Death is a lesson to learn about,
Death is a loss, without a doubt.

Musfirah Usman (11)
Excelsior Academy, Newcastle Upon Tyne

Equal Rights

Fight for the future
We know we can
How do you think girls and women feel that men get paid more than them?
People think girls have to cook, clean, but no, we don't
We can do jobs that men can do as well
Girls and women are strong, not just boys
All we want is for girls and women to get the same treatment as men and boys.

Terri Leigh Murray (13)
Excelsior Academy, Newcastle Upon Tyne

Stop Homophobia

H urtful words never leave
O ur hurting is always complete
M any people stare and shout
O n the bus and out
P eople laugh, people shout
H omophobia needs to stop
O nly some are kind
B eing me is lonely
I n the public and about
A lways be yourself.

Corey Burn (13)
Excelsior Academy, Newcastle Upon Tyne

Miss Trouble

Naughty, troublemaker, laughter
Always getting into fights at home and on my street
If you ever meet her
You will get into a fight if you mess with her
But if you see inside her
You might see a different person
Loud, laughter, smiler
Just getting into trouble for fussing
More like Little Miss Trouble.

Rosie Dickinson (11)
Excelsior Academy, Newcastle Upon Tyne

Bullying

B ullying is bad for mental health
U nderstanding that bullying is not okay
L eads to suicide
L eads to self-harm
Y ou should never let bullies bully you
I won't tolerate bullying
N o to bullying
G ood to understand that bullying can mess up people.

Mia Stevens (12)
Excelsior Academy, Newcastle Upon Tyne

Football

F ouling in football is not good
O wn goals are always an accident
O pportunities are endless
T ry different sports
B ecome better at your hobby
A lways play when you have an opportunity
L ove your hobby
L earn new skills.

Justin Lakatos (13)
Excelsior Academy, Newcastle Upon Tyne

The Bigger Picture

How come tons of plastic are thrown into the ocean every day?
Every single person should have a say.
This has to stop.
This has gone too far.
On the Earth it's leaving a scar.
The government needs to see the real picture,
As normal citizens are like an unknown figure.

Mohammed Ibrahim Komal (11)
Excelsior Academy, Newcastle Upon Tyne

Mr Calm

Loud, bad, chill
Always outthinks
And always on his bike
If you ever met him
You would be chill
But if you could see inside him
You would see a different person
Calm, quiet, always thinks of a way out
He just gets along with everyone
More like Mr Calm.

Muhammad-Ans Ali (11)
Excelsior Academy, Newcastle Upon Tyne

It's Just Not Fair

Tidy your room!
It's not even messy
Give me that phone!
But I'm not done with it
Put your shoes away!
Give me time to actually take them off
Get down and eat dinner now!
I'm not hungry.

It makes me feel like a raging volcano!

Ayesha Wilkinson (11)
Excelsior Academy, Newcastle Upon Tyne

Stop Fossil Fuels

Stop all fossil fuels,
This is so cruel,
There isn't a supply,
How long do we have to wait for a reply?

Carbon dioxide releasing into the atmosphere,
The planet is in fear,
How long do we have to protest?
I will be counting on my Rolex.

Ethan Taylor (11)
Excelsior Academy, Newcastle Upon Tyne

Miss Chatterbox

Loud, shy, funny
Always laughing, always listening
If you met her you would have a shock
But if you could see inside her you might see a different person
Quiet, not shy, chatterbox
Just getting on with it, never complaining
More like Miss Chatterbox.

Meike Sanci (11)
Excelsior Academy, Newcastle Upon Tyne

We Need To Stop This

R eally unfair because we can't stop this
A re you aware that you can stop it
C ome together, we will unite
I n this fight we won't stop this
S o we can overcome this
M e and you will come together and end this.

Kaleel Hassain (13)
Excelsior Academy, Newcastle Upon Tyne

Mr Loud

Friendly, good listener, sensible
Always fun, always bored
If you ever met him
You would be safe
But if you could see inside him
You might see a different person
Loud, silly, hyper
Just sometimes calm, sometimes shy
More like Mr Loud.

Filip Bari (11)
Excelsior Academy, Newcastle Upon Tyne

About Trash

We need help
To make our city beautiful
We need to tell people to stop throwing trash
Our city needs to be beautiful
Like other countries
To be nice
But we need people
To help us
For the city
To make it clean.

Darin Mariwan (13)
Excelsior Academy, Newcastle Upon Tyne

It's Just Not Fair

Put your coat on!
We aren't going out
Get off your Xbox!
I just got on
Get outside now!
But I just got back
You're late!
The door was locked
It makes me feel like a volcano.

Aiden Carr (12)
Excelsior Academy, Newcastle Upon Tyne

Racism

I sat down that night,
Looking at my night light,
Excited for school,
Thought I'd be cool.
I got ready that morning,
Couldn't stop yawning.
I finally reached the school,
Already starting to drool.
As I went through the gates,
I saw people laughing with their mates.
I was all lonely and scared,
But nobody cared.
I could hear people talking about me,
I was so dizzy that I couldn't even see.

I got bullied every day 'cause I'm a different race.
I had no choice, I was too scared to stick up for myself,
But now I realise I had made a mistake.
But now we shall all stick up for ourselves.
If you are the person who bullies everyone because of their race,
Or if you don't treat everyone the same,
Think of yourself,
How would you feel if you were getting bullied?
People can't choose the way they want to be,
So respect them.

Wanisa Wajid (11)
Green Oak Academy, Moseley

Climate Change Poem

Mother Nature does not object when you
Dump waste in her oceans,
She cannot scream when you cut down her trees,
That we as humans breathe,
She cannot cough when we pollute the
Air with greenhouse gases,
She cannot cry when you murder her animals
Just for us to eat and survive,
She cannot beseech them as we
Watch her Arctic melt and act like it's nothing,
She cannot open her mouth and speak about how much
We put her in pain but the evidence is ordinary to see,
Only if we could speak, make a change,
Everything would be back to normal,
If you as a human are not prepared to care about
The oceans, the trees, the animals, and the Earth,
If you're not willing to make a change for the future people,
If you're not willing to care,
What does that make you?

Sidrah Irshad (12)
Green Oak Academy, Moseley

Stop Hurting Yourself

I would like to say,
I'm not being heard at bay,
Most people around smoke,
And they do provoke other people. *Provoke!*
Why're you not listening?
You won't be glistening,
You're poisoning your lavish lungs,
You'll soon be as small as fungi,
You will become addicted,
Soon you'll be conflicted,
Your brain will long for smoking,
Unfortunately, you'll be choking,
Your brain'll be mushed,
You'll be catastrophically crushed,
So heed my warning,
Don't go off yawning,
You won't be listening to my speech,
But I want to ask you,
Is it worth the risk?

Amal Jama (11)
Green Oak Academy, Moseley

Racism

R acism was common around the world in the late nineteenth century.
A ll of mankind was sent to the penitentiary.
C ausing racism was one of the biggest diseases.
I ndicating racism was very common until Martin Luther King came.
S aviour of the coloured people, he insured everyone was treated fairly; no matter what they looked like.
M artin Luther King's quote was:

'Be a bush if you can't be a tree. If you can't be a highway, be a trail. If you can't be a sun, be a star. For it isn't by size that you win or fail. Be the best of whatever you are.'

Amina Chowdhury (12)
Green Oak Academy, Moseley

All About Anti-Bullying

A ll people should stand up for themselves
N ever be bullied
T hink before you speak
I should stand up for people.

B ullying
U nkind
L ies
L aughing at others
Y elling
I nconsiderate
N ame-calling
G oing around and telling rumours.

Seriously,
Don't bully people,
Be kind,
You can never know what's going on with their lives,
Maybe something bad.

Amina Bilal (11)
Green Oak Academy, Moseley

All About Racism

No matter what colour you are,
You will be a star,
No matter where you came to live,
For some people it is hard to forgive,
Even though you may feel you've done nothing wrong,
It will always be the same song,
"You don't belong here,"
"Stay well clear, don't come here,"
They shout in fear,
But I don't let it bother me.

No matter what colour you are,
You will always be a star!

Yasmin Begum (11)
Green Oak Academy, Moseley

Racism

R acism, racism, this has to stop.
A fter lives being taken, trying and trying, still no change to this pious world.
C apturing and judging black people while doing bigotry.
I will not let this happen, I will make a change.
S ome might say, "It's okay, it's okay," but, I won't let this rotate.
M ost of us are crying every night, but, some of us are dying every night.

Aleena Rehman (11)
Green Oak Academy, Moseley

Litter

Walking along the beach's warm sand
Holding a bucket and spade in my hand
What's that?
A plastic bag?
This belongs in the bin
Far away, not to hurt a creature's fin
I look around and all I see
Litter everywhere
As far as can be
Wondering what this world has become
Litter cannot be the main problem!

Safiyya Ali (11)
Green Oak Academy, Moseley

Global Warming

Global warming is somewhere soon
As we start to face our doom
Are we forgetting about trees and seas
Because we need to feel our hopes and dreams.

Let us help Mother Nature
Let us make a perfect structure
There are lots of reasons that we should live
The lovely Earth that we should fix.

In the trees there are birds and bees
Soon they won't have anywhere to flee
Life is important here on Earth
Don't let disaster strike.

So, wake up, wake up, time to say wake up
Hurry up, hurry up, time to clean up
Let it brighten up, let it brighten up
Let us make a brighter natural world.

Mathew Justin (12)
Oaklands Catholic School & Sixth Form College, Waterlooville

Global Warming

G lobal depression
L and sliding, killing people
O verfilling with corpses of trees
B lizzards raid houses
A valanches sliding with snow
L ightning zaps angrily.

W aves increasing
A s we face death
R aging earthquakes collide
M other Nature is angry at us
I am sad because of you
N ow you will suffer what I have suffered
G lobal death.

Jeswin Jaison (12)
Oaklands Catholic School & Sixth Form College, Waterlooville

Environment

Pollution, floods, climate change, fire,
Waste is growing, landfills getting higher.
Many, many things we can do,
But do you care about what's around you?
Together, a better world we can create,
So do your part before it's too late.
Reuse and recycle,
Walk, don't drive.
If everyone helps,
We'll stay alive.

Emilie Tredgold (11)
St Joan Of Arc Catholic School, Rickmansworth

Nature

A note of a bird and a song
Listen so closely or it may be gone
As you look at the bay you will notice the horizon
The sound of waves so sweet
You almost forget you have feet
Gushes of wind blowing to your face
Make you feel such grace
Let us not destroy our nature
And save it for all we care.

Senuli Godakandaarachchi (11)
St Joan Of Arc Catholic School, Rickmansworth

Monday Blues

Monday rolls around,
My head feels drowned,
It's the first day of school,
And I can't be bothered with the rules.

I'd rather be anywhere than here,
I can't wait for my last year,
School sucks the life out of me,
The best part of the day is when I'm free.

Riley Dixon (13)
The Heights Free School, Blackburn

Riding Through The Streets

My Sur-Ron is matte black,
I've got my charger in my rucksack,
I cruise through the streets,
Whilst I listen to the beats,
Got brand-new treads on my feet,
I'm looking very neat,
My mate's on the back seat,
While we speed on the concrete.

Kyle Cooper (14)
The Heights Free School, Blackburn

Surviving The Streets

People on crack,
The towns full of smack,
The boys like to get high,
But if their mums find out they'll cry,
They're all kitted out in ballies,
Dealing down the back allies,
How's a man supposed to survive,
When the world is so deprived?

Corey Marsden (14)
The Heights Free School, Blackburn

Blended

We are all living life on our socials,
The problem has become global.
Everyone is faking their identity,
All too wrapped up in their own vanity.
Society pushes us to be something we are not,
Blending our faces until we have been forgotten.

Mieka Whiteside (14)
The Heights Free School, Blackburn

Hope And Despair

We were promised that our lives would improve
But when we tried to help, they would all disapprove
And when things went wrong
They prompted us to be strong
Leaving everything for the next generation
To struggle to solve it in desperation
Poverty, war and pollution
Will we ever find a solution?
A fair, equal place where we could live in unity
Where we are all a close community
Well, it's just a dream
A dream with a calm, slice-of-life theme
And when we wake up from that fantasy
All I see is this world devolving into insanity
Our lives thrown into a state of disarray
While everyone else is telling us, "It's okay."

Suhailah Parvez (13)
William Perkin CE High School, Greenford

Dear Anxiety

Dear anxiety,
Ruining society.
What have you done to this world?

The crying,
The trying,
The thinking,
Distressing,
The worrying.
Do you not have better things to do?

Get out of our thoughts,
Get devoured by our powerful minds,
Which we struggle to keep in line.

People staring, glaring, comparing,
Bragging, snapping, trapping you,
Into a flood of problems that you completely do not need.
Yours sincerely, the world.

Arina Imyanitova (12)
William Perkin CE High School, Greenford

The Problem Of The World

Although the seasons change,
It doesn't feel so strange.
For when you look beyond nature,
You start to see the stubborn creature.

This creature has no name,
Discrimination is its game.
And though it is millenniums old,
Its stories are still being told.

Our society,
Is taken over by an evil entity.
Even when we try to speak against it,
There will always be someone supporting it.

Weronika Stanisz (14)
William Perkin CE High School, Greenford

Young Writers Information

We hope you have enjoyed reading this book – and that you will continue to in the coming years.

If you're the parent or family member of an enthusiastic poet or story writer, do visit our website **www.youngwriters.co.uk/subscribe** and sign up to receive news, competitions, writing challenges and tips, activities and much, much more! There's lots to keep budding writers motivated!

If you would like to order further copies of this book, or any of our other titles, then please give us a call or order via your online account.

Young Writers
Remus House
Coltsfoot Drive
Peterborough
PE2 9BF
(01733) 890066
info@youngwriters.co.uk

Join in the conversation!
Tips, news, giveaways and much more!

YoungWritersUK **YoungWritersCW** **youngwriterscw**